Jack and the Jungle

Malachy Doyle
Illustrated by Bryan Langdo

A & C Bl

White Wolves series consultant: Sue Ellis,
Centre for Literacy in Primary Education

This book can be used in the White Wolves Guided Reading
programme by readers of average ability in Year 2

First paperback edition 2011
First published 2010 by
A & C Black Publishers Ltd
36 Soho Square, London, W1D 3QY

www.acblack.com
www.malachydoyle.com

ISBN 978-1-4081-2211-2

A CIP catalogue for this book is available from the British Library.

This book is produced using paper that is made from wood
grown in managed, sustainable forests. It is natural, renewable
and recyclable. The logging and manufacturing processes conform
to the environmental regulations of the country of origin.

Printed and bound in China by C&C Offset Printing Co.

Chapter One

"I'm bored!" cried Jack.

He didn't like his new garden. There was nowhere to play. And no one to play with.

"I'M BORED!" he roared.

Then he saw a ball, lying on the grass.

He swung back his foot and knocked it against the wall.

But he kicked the ball too hard.

It went high, into the air...
It flew over the top of the wall, and
landed in the garden next door.

Only it wasn't a garden. He'd seen it from the house. It was full of trees and creepers, and it was more like a jungle!

"Oh no," said Jack. "It's probably full of wild animals. How am I going to get my ball back?"

He found a box and put it beside the wall. But it was too high to climb...

It was too high even to see over.
"Hello," said Jack. "Is anyone there?"
But there was no answer.

"Hello," he said, a bit louder. "Can I
have my ball back, please?"
There was still no answer.

Chapter Two

Suddenly, Jack heard a voice.

"Over here!" it said.

He looked around, but he couldn't see anyone.

"Up here!" cried the voice.

Jack looked up, into the trees. And saw a face, smiling down at him.

"Hi," said the face. "I'm Abbie."

It was a face full of freckles. Freckles and red hair.

"I'm Jack," said Jack.

"Have you seen my ball?
I kicked it over the wall, by mistake."

"No," said Abbie. "I was too busy chasing snakes. But I'll go and have a look for it, if you want."

Jack was worried. He didn't like snakes. They were all slimy, and sometimes they bit people.

He was going to tell Abbie not to worry about his ball, but she had disappeared.

He looked all around. He couldn't see her anywhere.

Then Abbie waved to him from another tree, further down the wall.

"I can see your ball, Jack," she called. "But I have some bad news for you…"

"What?" asked Jack.

"A wolf has got it!" said Abbie. "A deadly, dangerous wolf."

Chapter Three

Jack didn't know what to say.

"Stay there a minute," said Abbie. "I'll go and get it off him."

"Be careful," said Jack, under his breath. "Wolves bite."

Jack could hear Abbie fighting the wolf.
It was quite a struggle.

At last there was a thud, and the ball came through the trees.

It flew over the wall and bounced next to Jack. It nearly hit his dad's new greenhouse.

"I've sorted out the wolf!" cried Abbie, from deep within the jungle. "But there's more bad news…"

"Oh dear," said Jack. "What is it now?"

"Three tigers are coming towards me," she shouted. "Three tigers with very sharp teeth!"

"Oh no!" Jack covered his ears. He didn't want to hear her being eaten by a tiger.

"Abbie, Abbie, where are you?" he said, after a while. "Are you all right?"

"I'm fine," came the answer. "I escaped from the tigers, but..."

"But what?"

"But now there's a giant coming," said Abbie. "A great hungry giant!"

Chapter Four

"Help!" moaned Jack.

He crouched down behind the wall.
He stayed there for a long time. Everything
was silent. And he couldn't see a thing with
his eyes tight shut.

Suddenly, he heard a creaking sound.

A hand touched him on the shoulder and he nearly jumped out of his skin.

"It's all right, Jack," said a soft voice. "Follow me."

It was Abbie!

She showed him a door in the wall.

It was so hidden by spiky things that Jack hadn't seen it before.

Jack didn't really want to go into the jungle. But Abbie took him by the hand and led him through the door.

She was whistling!

Trees and tall grasses pressed in, all around them.

Jack kept his eyes on the ground to make sure he didn't stand on a snake.

But he had to look up, every now and again, in case there were any wolves or tigers or giants.

Chapter Five

At last, they came to the edge of the jungle.

In front of them was a pond. A woman was sitting on the other side. She was laying out a picnic on the grass. Beside her were a dog and three cats.

The dog came bounding over, wagging its tail.

"Guess who this is, Jack…" said Abbie, laughing.

Jack didn't know what to say.

"It's the WOLF!" cried Abbie. "And guess who these are," she said, pointing at the cats.

"The three tigers?" said Jack.

Abbie nodded. "This is the GIANT..." she said, pointing to the woman.

"And this is the SNAKE!" she cried,
picking up a hosepipe and spraying water
all over him.

"Hello, Jack. I'm Abbie's mum," said the giant, smiling. "I hope my daughter hasn't been teasing you."

"Sorry, Jack," said Abbie, grinning. "But I only tease people I like."

Jack sat down in the sunshine to dry off.

The giant gave him some lemonade and a big slice of carrot cake.

The wolf licked his face.

The tigers curled up on his lap, and Jack was happy.

It was only the first day in his new house and already he'd found a friend. A friend and a jungle full of animals!